W9-BFH-412

The CASE of the
MISSING CANARY

Written by Robyn Supraner

Illustrated by Robbie Stillerman

Troll Associates

Copyright © 1979 by Troll Associates
All rights reserved. No part of this book may be used or reproduced
in any manner whatsoever without written permission from the publisher.
Printed in the United States of America.

Troll Associates, Mahwah, N.J.

Library of Congress Catalog Card Number: 78-60122

The CASE of the MISSING CANARY

The first time Patty wore her new glasses, everyone had something to say.

"You look older," said T.G.

"You look smarter," said Annie.

"You look funny," said Wilbur.

"How would you like a knuckle sandwich?" asked Patty.

"May I try them on?" asked T.G.
Patty shook her head.
"Why not?" asked T.G.
"Because," said Patty.
"Because why?" asked T.G.

"Because," said Patty. "They're magic."

"Ha!" said Wilbur. "Ha! Ha! Ha!"

"Laugh all you like," said Patty. "I don't care."

She picked up her cat, White Toe, and rubbed the cat's head. White Toe purred. "Cats are smart," said Patty. "White Toe believes in magic. Don't you, White Toe?"

"Meow," said White Toe.

"See," said Patty.

"Are they *really* magic?" asked Annie.

"Of course," said Patty. "I can see everything with these glasses. I can see a mouse in its house, five miles away."

"Ha!" said Wilbur.

"What else can you see?" asked Annie.

"I can see a frog on a log in the fog, on Maple Street," said Patty.

"Haw!" said Wilbur.

3

"What else can you see?" asked Annie.

"I can see that White Toe has exactly fifty-one billion, seven hundred and forty-six hairs," said Patty. "Not counting his whiskers, of course."

"Liar!" said Wilbur.

"Count them for yourself, if you don't

believe me," said Patty. "These glasses can
see everything."

Wilbur shook his head. "Do you know
what you are?" he asked. "You are the
world's biggest liar!"

"How would you like a free trip to the
moon?" asked Patty.

"I believe Patty," said Annie. "I believe she is telling the truth. Aren't you, Patty?"

Before Patty could answer, she heard her mother call, "Patricia, Theodore, come inside, at once!"

"Uh-oh," said Patty. "Here comes trouble."

"How can you tell?" asked Wilbur.

"When my mother calls me Patricia . . ." said Patty.

"And when she calls me Theodore . . ." said T.G.

"It means big trouble," finished Patty.

Patty and T.G. went inside. Annie and Wilbur went, too.

Mrs. Jinks was very upset. She pointed
to the canary's cage. The door was open. The
cage was empty. "Popcorn is missing," said
Mrs. Jinks. "Have any of you seen him?"

Patty shook her head.

Annie shook her head.

Wilbur shook his head.

T.G. shook his head.

"Does anyone know who left the cage door open?" asked Mrs. Jinks.

Patty, Annie, and Wilbur shook their heads.

T.G. did not shake his head.

"Well," said his mother. "I'm waiting, T.G."

"Well," said T.G. "It was like this. Today is my day to feed Popcorn and change his water. Which, you will be very happy to know, I did."

"And?" said his mother.

"And," said T.G. "I thought Popcorn would like some nice, fresh air."

"So?" said his mother.

"So," said T.G. "I opened the door to his cage."

"You *what*?" said his mother.

"I made a mistake," said T.G.

"Boy, are you dumb!" said Patty. "Popcorn's cage is full of fresh air. It comes in through the bars. You are really dumb!"

Wilbur patted T.G. on the shoulder.
"Don't worry," he said. "Patty will find
Popcorn. Remember? She can see everything
through her magic glasses. Isn't that right,
Patty?"

"How would you like to swing on a star?" asked Patty.

"Come on, Patty," said T.G. "You said your glasses were magic. Now prove it."

"Did I say I couldn't find Popcorn?" asked Patty. "Did I say that?"

"No," said T.G.

"No," said Annie.

"Not yet," said Wilbur.

"So what's all the fuss about? I will find
Popcorn for you. I promise. But first, I must
ask myself a magical question."

"What question?" asked T.G.

Patty stared through her glasses. "The

question is this," she said. "If I were a
canary, where would I hide?"

"That's a great question," said Annie.

"We don't need great questions,"
complained Wilbur. "We need great
answers."

"I know where I would hide," said T.G.
"I would hide in a closet."

"Canaries can't open closet doors,"
sniffed Annie.

"I meant an *open* closet," said T.G.

"We'll see," said Patty. She opened a closet and looked inside.

"Hey!" said Annie. "Aren't those my skates? I thought you said you gave them back!"

"What's this!" yelled Wilbur. "My *Super Hero* comic books! I thought you said you gave them back!"

"Is that my butterfly net?" asked T.G. "I thought you said you gave it back!"

"My magic tells me this is the wrong place to look," said Patty. She slammed the closet door.

"Shhhhhhh!" whispered Annie. "Listen!"

They listened. This is what they heard.

Tweeee tweeeeeee tweeeeeeeeee-e-e-e.

The sound was coming from the kitchen.

"It's Popcorn!" shouted Annie. "I heard him first!"

"I heard him second!" yelled T.G.

"Come on!" shouted Wilbur.

"Be quiet!" whispered Patty. "Do you want to scare him to death?"

They tiptoed into the kitchen. Very, very quietly.

TWEEEE TWEEEEEEEEEE TWEEEEEEEEEEEEE-E-E-E.

The sound was getting louder.

"Rats!" said T.G.
"It's only the tea kettle."

"If I were a canary," said Wilbur, "I
would fly up in the air. I would fly around
until I saw a tree. Then I would rest."

"The coat tree!" said T.G. "Come on!"

There was a sweater on the coat tree.
There was a hat on the coat tree. There was
even a coat on the coat tree. But there was
no canary.

"Poor little Popcorn," said Annie. "If I were a canary, I would fly back into my cage. I would be afraid that a mean old cat would come and eat me up."

"A mean old cat!" cried Wilbur. "Has anyone seen White Toe?"

Nobody had. Nobody knew where she was. They looked everywhere. But they could not find her. White Toe and Popcorn were both missing. They were missing, together!

They all called: "Here kitty, kitty, kitty!"

They all coaxed: "Come, pretty White
Toe. Good, kind, beautiful White Toe!"
They offered her cream. "Here's cream
for you, kitty. Sweet, delicious cream!"
But White Toe did not come.

Then they heard a different sound.
Scritch. Scratch. Scritch. Scratch.
The sound was coming from the closet.
"It's White Toe!" cried Wilbur. "We
locked her in the closet!"

They opened the closet door. There, sitting on the shelf, her tail wound neatly around her, was White Toe. In her mouth was a small yellow feather!

"Oh, White Toe!" cried Wilbur. "What have you done?"

Annie covered her eyes. "Is Popcorn all eaten up?" she cried. "Oh, I can't look!"

"Oh, what have I done! Forgive me, Popcorn!" cried T.G. "I will never, never, *ever* leave your cage door open again!"

"Hold it!" said Patty. "Hold it right there! I am getting a magical message!"

"It's too late," said Wilbur. "It's too late for magic."

Patty did not listen. She walked to the window. It was open. The sounds of birds and bees, chirping and buzzing, came into the house.

"If I were a canary," said Patty, "I
would wonder about the world outside. I
would wonder about the sky and the trees. I
would wonder about other birds. If I were a
canary, I would fly away . . . into the world."

"But what about the feather in White Toe's mouth?" asked Wilbur.

"That feather was from my father's hat," said Patty.

"Oh," said Annie. "I'm so glad!"

"And now," said Patty, "my magic

glasses tell me that Popcorn is in the
garden."

The children ran outside. They heard the
wind. They heard the bees. They heard the
robin's song. Then they heard a very special
sound.

Chireeeeeee Chireeeeeeeee Chirrrrrrup.

"It's Popcorn!" cried T.G. "He's saying cheer up!"

"I hear him!" cried Wilbur.

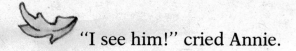

"I see him!" cried Annie.

Popcorn was sitting on a lilac bush. He
was sunning himself and enjoying the world.

When he saw Patty, he flew to her and rested on her finger. He cocked his head and whistled. He seemed to be saying:

Now that I have seen the world, I am ready to come home.

When Popcorn was safe in his cage, Patty said, "They work every time."

"What?" asked Annie. "What works?"

"My magic glasses, of course," said Patty. "My magic glasses and my great brain."

"Tell me the truth," said Annie. "Are your glasses really magic?"

"Not really," said Patty. "I made that part up. But the other part is true. I really have a great brain!"

"Patty!" said Annie.

"What did I tell you?" said Wilbur.

"Who cares?" said T.G. He hugged his sister. "Brains are better than magic, any day!"